Super Pig's Adventures

and
Jip the Pirate

Illustrated by Nina O'Connell

CONTENTS

Super Pig's Adventures   2

Jip the Pirate   9

STECK-VAUGHN
COMPANY

Super Pig's Adventures

Look at me.

I am Super Pig.

I am going to Deb's party.

Tom sat down to wait

for Sam and Meg.

He went to sleep. Zzzzzz.

Look at me.
What can I see?
I can see Sam.
I will help him.
I am Super Pig!

3

Look at me.
What can I see?
Jip is in the fire.
I will help him.
Here comes Super Pig!

Look at me.
What can I see?
I can see Ben.
I will help him.
I am Super Pig!

Look at me.
What can I see?
I can see Deb.
I will help her.
I am Super Pig!

What can I see now?

There is Meg.

I will help her.

Here comes Super Pig!

Come on, Tom.
Get up!
It is time to go
to Deb's party!

Jip the Pirate

Jip was going to Deb's party.

"I will be a pirate," he said.

"I will have a red coat.

I will have a big hat.

I will have big boots."

Jip sat down to wait for
Tom and Ben and Meg.
He went to sleep.
Zzzzzz. Zzzzzz. Zzzzzz.

Jip was on a pirate ship.

The ship had a pirate flag.

The pirates had a map.

They wanted to find the gold.

"Where is the gold?" asked Jip.

"I don't know," said Meg.

"You must ask Ben."

"Where is the gold?" asked Jip.

"I don't know," said Ben.

"You must ask Tom."

"Where is the gold?" asked Jip.
"I don't know," said Tom.

"Then you must **all** walk the plank!"
said Jip.
"Ready! Set! Go!"

Bang! Bang! Bang!

"Come on, Jip," said Meg.

"Get up!

It is time to go to the party!"